A BAD DAY FOR JAYDEN

TONY BRADMAN

Illustrated by
TANIA REX

Barrington Stoke

First published in 2020 in Great Britain by
Barrington Stoke Ltd
18 Walker Street, Edinburgh, EH3 7LP

www.barringtonstoke.co.uk

Text © 2020 Tony Bradman
Illustrations © 2020 Tania Rex

A CIP catalogue record for this book is available
from the British Library upon request

ISBN: 978-1-78112-901-2

Printed in China by Leo

For all the Jaydens and
Miss Wilsons everywhere

CONTENTS

CHAPTER 1

The First Surprise

BEEP-BEEP-BEEP!

Jayden had been awake for a long time when his alarm went off. He always woke up early and didn't go back to sleep. His clock was old, and Jayden never knew if it was going to work. He spent half the night checking it and getting worried. He waited for it to go off. *That's why I'm always so tired*, he thought. He didn't have a phone yet. "When you go to secondary school," his mum said.

He hit the alarm's off button, got out of bed and pulled back his curtains. Rain was falling from the grey sky onto the street outside the block of flats where he lived. It wasn't yet seven o'clock but people were already standing at the bus stop. There was lots of traffic too, cars and vans swishing along the wet road.

Jayden headed for the bathroom and brushed his teeth. Then he went back to his bedroom and quickly got dressed. Mum hadn't done any clothes washing for a while, so he would have to wear the same clothes as the day before. That would be OK for a bit – it was only his school uniform. But he didn't want to wear the same clothes for three or even four days ...

Maybe Mum would do the washing today. They really needed some shopping as well – the fridge was almost empty. He wanted to ask Mum if he should go to the shop, but he'd have to wake her up first.

Their flat was small, with just two bedrooms, a front room, a tiny kitchen and an even more tiny bathroom. His little sister Madison had the big bedroom. She had more stuff than him – soft toys and dolls and things like that. Mum didn't have a bedroom. She slept in the front room on a sofa-bed, and Jayden knew it wasn't very comfy.

Madison's door was half open, and Jayden saw that she was still in bed, fast asleep. The front-room door was closed, and Jayden opened it softly. Mum was on the sofa, under an old duvet. Jayden could only see the very top of her head.

"Mum?" he said. "Are you awake? It's morning, time to get up."

"What?" Mum said from under the duvet. "Oh, leave me alone, Jayden ..."

Jayden gave a sigh. Mum had been in a funny mood ever since she'd lost her job at the supermarket. Jayden thought she'd be upset, maybe angry, but instead it was like she'd shut down. She hardly ever left the flat and spent most of her time sitting around. She wasn't looking for another job, so Jayden worried about what would happen if they ran out of money. They'd never had much in the first place.

"OK, Mum," Jayden said, and he backed slowly out of the room. Mum pulled the duvet right over her head, and now he couldn't see anything of her at all.

Jayden got on with what he had to do. He woke Madison, then made her have a wash and get dressed. She was grumpy in the mornings and it took a while.

At last she was ready, and Jayden gave her something to eat. There was just enough cornflakes and milk for her. Jayden had the last two slices of bread. They were old and a

bit stale, but he spread lots of Marmite over them.

He didn't know what they'd have for dinner later. There wasn't anything left.

"What's wrong with Mum?" said Madison. They were both sitting at the little table in the kitchen. "Why hasn't she got up again?"

"Er … she hasn't been feeling very well," said Jayden. Madison stared at him. Her bottom lip began to wobble, and he thought she was going to cry. "Don't worry, she'll be all right," he added quickly. "Come on, we need to leave or we'll be late for school."

He sent her to put on her shoes and coat, and went to check on Mum. She hadn't moved, so he went to put on his shoes and coat too. "Bye, Mum!" he called out from the hall, trying to sound cheerful for Madison. "We're off now, see you later!"

There was no answer, and Jayden nearly sighed again. But Madison was looking at him with big eyes, and he held it in. He opened the front door, made sure his key was in his pocket, then led his sister down the two flights of stairs and out onto the street.

It was only a short walk to school along the main road. There was more traffic now, but at least the rain had stopped. The school gates were as busy as always – grown-ups dropping kids off, the kids meeting up in the playground. Madison was in Year Two, and she ran straight over to her friends by the Infants entrance. She seemed a bit happier now, not so worried, Jayden thought, and that was good.

Jayden spotted his best friend Dylan across the playground and went over to him. Most days they met up before they had to go in with their Year Six class. Sometimes they played football, but often they just laughed and joked and messed around.

"Hey, Dylan," he said, expecting Dylan to grin and give him a fist-bump.

Dylan was talking to Luca, one of the other boys in their class. Jayden had never much liked Luca. He thought that Dylan felt the same. So what happened next was a surprise – the first of Jayden's day – and not a very nice one.

"Go away, Jayden," said Dylan, scowling. "We're not friends any more."

Then Dylan and Luca walked off, arms round each other.

Jayden watched them go, his heart sinking.

Why wasn't Dylan his friend any more?

CHAPTER 2
New Teacher

Just then, the supply teacher for Jayden's class hurried through the gates and into the playground. Her name was Miss Wilson, and the day hadn't started well for her, either. It was her first day at the school, and she'd been keen to get there on time. But the bus had been late, and in the end it had all been a bit of a rush.

She stood still for a second to catch her breath and work out where she should go. The school building was old and definitely needed a bit of care and attention. The paint was dirty and cracked. There were some run-down huts on one side of the playground. They looked like big garden sheds, but they were classrooms.

The children looked happy enough. Just like at any school, they came in all shapes and sizes. Some stood in small groups talking, while others ran around, chasing each other or playing football. Miss Wilson spotted a boy standing on his own. He had curly dark hair and a nice face, but he looked unhappy, and she wondered why ...

Miss Wilson sighed and shook her head – she should get a move on. She saw a sign saying, "All visitors MUST report to School Office", with a big arrow pointing to double doors. That would be her best bet, she thought, and soon she was standing at the office counter, telling one of the secretaries who she was.

It was very noisy, and the secretary couldn't hear what Miss Wilson was saying. Another secretary was arguing with a parent – something about a letter that should have been signed and wasn't. At last Miss Wilson explained why she was there, and a few moments later she was taken into the staff room. It was crowded with teachers drinking tea and coffee and talking. Mrs Green, the Head, was sitting in the corner, frowning as she hunched over a laptop.

"Ah, thank goodness you're here at last!" said Mrs Green, looking up at her.

"Sorry I didn't get here sooner," said Miss Wilson. "The bus was late and—"

"Well, it's just one of those things," said Mrs Green. "You're lucky your class will be in an Assembly first thing this morning, so I can give you a proper tour."

Mrs Green snapped the laptop shut and put it to one side. She jumped to her feet and walked out of the staff room, then along the school's main corridor, which was packed with children. Miss Wilson tried her best to keep up with her, but it wasn't easy. Mrs Green was tall, and she walked very quickly. The children got out of her way, like the sea parting before a great ship, thought Miss Wilson.

"It's a big school, and we have a real mix of children," said Mrs Green. Miss Wilson noticed that the inside of the building was just as shabby as the outside. "They're all lovely, of course," Mrs Green went on. "But some can be rather, er ... tricky, to say the least. I'm sure you've seen it all before ..."

You can say that again, thought Miss Wilson. These days it felt as if she had been a teacher for way too long. She had definitely met a lot of kids – the bright and the dozy, the loud and the quiet, the tell-tales and those who liked to keep everything to themselves. She had met plenty of badly behaved kids, some with real problems. And once she had even met a boy who was too well behaved for his own good.

Miss Wilson had helped him and done the same for lots of others. That was one of the reasons she had become a teacher in the first place. She'd wanted to teach kids, but she had also wanted to make a difference to their lives. Yet things had changed, and over the last few years she had seemed to spend all her time filling out forms and getting the children ready to take tests. And that made her feel cross and sad.

Now Miss Wilson wasn't sure she wanted to be a teacher any more. But she didn't know what else she might do, and she couldn't afford to stop working. So she got a job filling in at different schools. She took the place of a teacher who was ill or having a baby. Being a supply teacher was much easier, mostly because she knew she would be moving on. It also gave her a chance to think about her future.

"This is where you'll be," said Mrs Green as they stopped by a classroom door at last. "I do hope you get on with them. We really need someone to be their teacher till the end of the school year at least. See how you get on today and let me know if you're interested."

"I'm not sure I can commit myself for that long ..." said Miss Wilson.

"Ah well, not to worry," said Mrs Green. "See you in the staff room at morning play, if you survive that long ... Just kidding!"

I've heard that one before, thought Miss Wilson as Mrs Green walked away. Then Miss Wilson went into the classroom. It looked like all the other classrooms she'd been in – the teacher's desk with a computer, a big screen for the class to look at, clusters of tables and chairs, shelves of books, displays on the walls. She saw straight away that the class topic this term was the Vikings – there were pictures of Viking longships and the Norse gods and goddesses.

The children arrived a few moments later. "Hello, Miss!" said one of the boys as the children came in and sat down, staring at her. "Are you our new teacher? You've got to be better than Miss Jenkins – she was rubbish. My name is Luca, by the way."

"Yes, that's right," said Miss Wilson. "And my name is Miss Wilson ..."

She was going to keep an eye on Luca. The boy she had spotted in the playground on his own was in this class too. He was sitting at a table near her.

When he saw her looking at him, he looked away.

CHAPTER 3
Left Out

Jayden's day wasn't getting any better. The Assembly had been in the hall, everyone sitting cross-legged on the floor. Luca had sat next to Dylan, where Jayden always sat. Until that moment, Jayden had thought Dylan might forget what he'd said before school, that they'd laugh and be friends again. But when Jayden saw Dylan sitting with Luca, he knew it was no joke. Luca even turned round to grin at him.

It hadn't been a cheerful Assembly either. One of the Year Five classes was doing

Climate Change as their topic, and they talked about all the bad things that were happening to the planet. It was an important subject, of course, and Jayden tried to listen. But his mind kept slipping back to his own problems. He kept worrying about if Mum had got up and if she was going to start looking for a job, or if she'd done the washing ...

Then there was the problem with Dylan. Jayden tried hard to think of what he might have done to make his best friend cross with him. True, he hadn't been round to Dylan's flat after school in a while. And he couldn't remember the last time Dylan had come round to his flat. But that couldn't be why Dylan didn't want to be friends, could it? Dylan knew about Mum, and how difficult things were – Jayden had told him.

And why did it have to be Luca that Dylan was friends with now? They had always laughed about Luca's non-stop brags. His mum and dad had a fancy house and a big car, and Luca had all the latest stuff. He often secretly brought expensive things to school, even though they weren't allowed – a tablet, a phone, a new game. It was easy to see that Luca only cared about himself, and Jayden had thought Dylan knew that too.

After the Assembly Jayden's class went to their classroom. A new teacher was waiting for them. Jayden had forgotten that Mrs Green had told them they would be getting a new teacher. Their class teacher this year, Miss Jenkins, was having a baby and she was going to leave at the end of term, but her baby had come a bit early. Miss Wilson had a nice face, but she didn't seem all that happy.

Jayden frowned when Luca said Miss Jenkins had been a rubbish teacher. She hadn't been that bad, just a bit tired and she sometimes forgot things, especially in the last few weeks. Luca and some of the others in the class hadn't been very nice to her, and she'd lost her temper with them a few times. Jayden had done his best to stay out of it. He had felt sorry for Miss Jenkins, and he hoped she would be all right.

"OK, children," said Miss Wilson. "Let's start with some Maths ..."

A few of them groaned, and Jayden felt as if his tummy had tied itself into a knot. Until this year he had always been good at his school work. But these days he just couldn't seem to keep his mind on what he was doing in class, and he never had time to do his homework at home. So he wasn't one of the clever kids any more, and Miss Jenkins had moved him to the table with the other dozy dimwits. At least that's what Luca had called them. And he'd kept saying it till Miss Jenkins had told him off.

Miss Wilson handed out worksheets, and soon everyone was working at them silently. Everyone except Jayden. He answered a few questions, then got stuck. He stared at the worksheet. He frowned, he shifted in his chair, he sighed.

"Are you OK?" whispered the boy beside him. "Do you need help?"

The boy's name was Olufemi, and he had joined the class a few weeks ago. He was very friendly and told good jokes, but Jayden hadn't taken much notice of him.

"You can't do that!" whispered a girl from the other side of the table. Her name was Kasia, and she liked things to be done properly. "It's cheating."

"Not if it's me who helps him," said Miss Wilson. "Let me have a look ..."

Miss Wilson showed Jayden what to do, but he felt himself blushing. The rest of the class must be looking at him, and he really didn't like it. Especially when he knew everyone thought he was stupid.

Then it was morning play, and Miss Wilson sent the class out into the playground. Jayden watched Dylan and Luca run off together and start playing football with some of the other boys. After a while he went over to join in, but Luca rounded on him

"We don't want you to play with us," said Luca. The others laughed.

"Why not?" Jayden answered, looking at Dylan.

"Because you're just so boring, Jayden," said Dylan. "All you do is talk about your mum being fed up and how you have to do everything for her."

Jayden didn't know what to say. He looked at Dylan for a moment, and the other boys stared at them both. Luca grinned, and then they all started playing football again, running past Jayden as if he wasn't there. Jayden turned and walked away.

Olufemi said something to him, but Jayden kept going. He ended up in a far corner of the playground and stayed there until it was time to go in again. He had been going to check on Madison, but he saw her playing with her friends in the Infants playground, and she was OK.

Jayden wasn't OK. He felt bad, thinking of all the times he'd gone on to Dylan about his mum. He should have worked it out for himself – Dylan wasn't interested in that stuff.

But then he thought, *Some friend Dylan turned out to be ...*

And now Jayden felt angry.

CHAPTER 4

Getting to Know Jayden

At that moment, Miss Wilson was in the staff room, making herself some tea in a chipped old mug that said "World's Best Teacher" on it. There was the same buzz of chatter as there had been before school, the other teachers talking, laughing or having a bit of a moan. But Miss Wilson couldn't stop thinking about Jayden.

He just seemed so unhappy, and that wasn't right for a child of his age.

"I see you survived, then," said Mrs Green. "How are you getting on?"

"Oh, not too badly," said Miss Wilson, sitting down beside her. "They seem like a nice bunch of kids, so far at least. But I wanted to ask you about Jayden."

"You'll have to remind me who he is," said Mrs Green, frowning. "There was a time when I'd have known every child in the school, but these days I'm too busy ..."

"He doesn't stand out," said Miss Wilson. "About the same height as the other Year Six boys, curly hair, nice face. But he looks worried all the time. I haven't seen him smile once all morning."

"Yes, I think I remember him now," said Mrs Green. "He has a little sister called Madison in Year Two. But he was always such a bright, cheerful boy."

"Madison is in my class," said another teacher, Miss Patel. "Their parents split up just before Christmas, and I don't think they've seen their dad for a while."

"Ah, that would explain it ..." Mrs Green said sadly, and they all nodded.

This was something else Miss Wilson had often seen before. Most people seemed to think Home and School were two completely separate worlds. But she knew that what happened in one could definitely affect the other. If you were struggling at school, then you'd probably be unhappy at home. And if there was stuff going on at home that made you unhappy, then you'd have a bad time at school.

Miss Wilson wanted to ask more questions about Jayden, but she didn't get a chance. Another teacher came over to ask Mrs Green about some problem, and Miss Patel was called out to deal with a girl in her class who had been sick.

So instead, Miss Wilson went back to her classroom. The children were still in the playground, and she looked through Miss Jenkins' files about them. *Miss Jenkins must have been a good teacher*, thought Miss Wilson. Her computer files were well organised and easy to follow, so Miss Wilson soon found what she was looking for – Jayden's marks and test scores for the year. They told an interesting story.

Jayden had started the year well. Then, halfway through the autumn, things had changed. His marks and test scores started to fall, and he stopped doing his homework. It was the same after Christmas, and Miss Jenkins had made a note to ask his mum to come in for a chat. But it looked like she hadn't got round to it before her baby had decided to arrive, and Miss Wilson couldn't blame her for that.

Poor Jayden, thought Miss Wilson. Of course she had no idea what he'd been going through at home, but she could see it was having an effect. There wasn't much she could do for him though, was there? He and his sister probably wanted their mum and dad to get back together again, but Miss Wilson couldn't make that happen. She wasn't the Fairy Godmother with a magic wand. She was just a teacher ...

Miss Wilson sighed and closed the tests and scores pages on the computer. She heard the bell ring in the playground, and soon the children came in, most of them full of life and chattering after their play-time. Jayden trailed in last, after everyone else, and she saw straight away that there was something different about him. He'd looked sad and worried before, but now he was scowling with anger.

"Are you all right, Jayden?" she said softly as he sat down in his place.

"Oh, don't worry about him, Miss," said Luca with a sneer. Some of the other boys sniggered.

"He's just grumpy because we wouldn't let him play with us."

"That doesn't sound very nice, Luca," said Miss Wilson. "Why not?"

"We don't like him, Miss," said Luca with a shrug, as if he almost wanted her to tell him off.

Everybody else was staring at Jayden now. *That's not good*, thought Miss Wilson. She could see he was blushing and looking even more angry.

"Well, Luca," said Miss Wilson, "I don't want to hear anything else like that from you today, do you understand? Right, who can tell me about your topic?"

Luca looked at her with a bit more respect and nodded. Lots of hands went up, and soon the children were talking over each other, explaining the work they had done. But then Miss Wilson knew children always enjoyed doing the Vikings.

Jayden, however, didn't join in. He sat with his head down, almost as if he wasn't part of the class at all. After a while Miss Wilson told the children to write a Viking story using everything they had learned. The class quickly grew quiet, everyone working away. Miss Wilson walked round, looking at their work. Some of it was good, and some not so good, which was no surprise.

Jayden didn't write very much at all and spent most of his time staring out of the window or at the clock. Miss Wilson began to think Luca and the other boys might be bullying him. She would have to watch out for that.

But then at lunch play something bad happened, and she didn't have to.

CHAPTER 5

The Second Surprise

Jayden could feel the anger growing inside him all morning, like lava in a volcano. He knew he should calm down. But it wasn't easy – he had so much to be angry about.

Why was everything going wrong? The problems had begun when Dad left, but Jayden knew there was nothing he could do about that. His parents weren't going to get on if they didn't want to, even if it was rubbish for him and Madison. Now Dylan wasn't his friend any more, and Luca was really enjoying being horrible to him.

Jayden sighed and tried to concentrate. By the time the bell went for lunch he had written a page. He felt a bit less angry as he joined the lunch queue in the hall. Madison was already there with her class. He saw her hand over her voucher to Mrs Ashby, the dinner lady, then take her tray to a table where some other Year Two children were sitting.

Luca and Dylan sat at that table too. They opened their packed lunches, and Luca was soon boasting to Dylan about the things his mum had put in his lunchbox.

"It's much better for me than that muck," Luca said with a nod at Madison's tray. "But you can't expect anything good when you're on free school meals …"

Then Luca said something else to Madison that Jayden couldn't hear. Madison looked at

Luca, and Jayden could tell she was upset – her bottom lip began to wobble. Now Jayden could feel his anger starting to bubble up again.

It was true – he and Madison were on free school meals. Everybody knew who the Free-School-Meals kids were. To begin with Jayden had felt embarrassed. He and Madison might as well have worn badges that said "Our Family Is So Broke!" But that had worn off because nobody said anything.

Until today, when Luca had to open his big mouth and upset his sister.

Jayden stepped out of the queue and went over to where Madison was sitting. He wasn't going to let Luca be horrible to her as well. She already had enough to put up with.

"Leave my sister alone, Luca," said Jayden. "Or else."

"Oooh, I'm so scared," said Luca, standing up. "Or else what, Jayden?"

Dylan was sitting there looking unhappy, as if he knew that Luca had gone way too far this time. But Luca was grinning, and Jayden just couldn't bear it any more. The volcano inside him suddenly boiled up to bursting point … and erupted.

Jayden pushed Luca hard in the chest with both hands. Luca stepped back, tripped over a chair and fell against the table. It crashed over and knocked against another table. Lunchboxes, trays and food, water jugs and cups all went flying.

Madison screamed, Luca jumped up and pushed Jayden back, and soon the two of them were punching each other on the floor, rolling around in the mess. Everyone in the hall rushed over to watch; some of them were chanting "FIGHT! FIGHT!"

"What on earth is going on?" somebody said at last in a very loud voice.

It was Mrs Green, and she wasn't happy. She had heard the noise from her office and had come to see what was going on, and now the hall fell totally silent. Mrs Ashby and two of the other dinner ladies got hold of Jayden and Luca and pulled them apart.

"He started it, Miss!" said Luca. "I was just sitting there, eating my lunch ..."

Mrs Green looked at Luca with a stern face. "Yes, well, if I had a pound for every time you told me something wasn't your fault, Luca, I'd be rich and I wouldn't have to work so hard any more," said Mrs Green. "Right, my office now, both of you."

She marched off and Luca followed, but Jayden wanted to check on Madison. Mrs Ashby had her arm round her, and she seemed OK, so he followed Mrs Green too. By the time they arrived at her office, his anger had vanished and he felt worried instead. He hated being in trouble or getting told off, and Mrs Green was very cross. She sat behind her desk and they stood in front of it, waiting for her to speak.

"You boys know that fighting isn't allowed in my school," she said at last. "I should keep both of you in my office this afternoon, and I'll be having a word with your parents ..."

Luca didn't seem bothered, but Jayden really didn't like the sound of that. He had a nasty feeling it might make his mum feel even more fed up, and that wasn't going to help. He felt sick with worry.

Just then Miss Wilson came in and stood to one side of Mrs Green's desk.

"Thanks for joining us, Miss Wilson," said Mrs Green. "These two boys from your class were fighting in the hall. What do you think I should do with them?"

Miss Wilson didn't speak for a moment,
and Jayden felt worse. He had been having a
seriously bad day, and what Miss Wilson said
next could make it much worse. But then she
gave him the second surprise of his day – she
smiled.

"I think you should let me deal with Luca and Jayden," she said. Jayden saw how Mrs Green gave him a careful look when Miss Wilson said his name. "I'm sure they're not really bad boys, they've just been a bit silly," Miss Wilson went on. "And if you do have to keep them in your office this afternoon, it will be hard for you to get on with all your work."

"Thank you, Miss Wilson," said Mrs Green. "Off you go with your teacher, boys ..."

And that afternoon, Jayden got the third surprise of his day.

CHAPTER 6

Talking

Miss Wilson took Luca and Jayden to the hall and handed them over to Mrs Ashby, who made them clean up the mess they had made. They finished their lunches, and then Miss Wilson took them back to the classroom and told them to sit down. She looked at them both and decided to deal with Luca first.

"I don't know what's been going on," she started. Luca opened his mouth to speak, but Miss Wilson held up her hand to silence him. "But I'm sure you're as much to blame as

Jayden, Luca, and I won't have boys in my class behaving like that ..."

She had met quite a few boys like Luca in her time, and she knew how to handle them. They weren't bad, just a bit full of themselves. Luca needed someone to be firm with him and make him see that he wasn't actually the centre of the world. He soon seemed to work out that she wouldn't take any nonsense from him anyway. Then she gave Jayden his telling-off too, and told the boys to say sorry to each other.

"You can go out to play now, Luca," she said, and he ran off. Jayden looked at her. He didn't know why she hadn't let him go out to play too. "You can go in a minute, Jayden, but can we have a chat first?"

"Er ... what about, Miss?" His face was full of worry again. "I swear I haven't done anything else, and I promise I won't get in any more fights, cross my heart."

"Relax, Jayden." Miss Wilson smiled. "Look, I know things might have been, well, a bit difficult for you at home, and sometimes it can help just to talk about it ..."

She waited a moment. Jayden was suddenly sitting very still, staring at her, eyes wide, and she knew she had to be careful – she didn't want him to clam up. She could see he was thinking hard, his face changing as he thought about what to say next.

"It's my mum, Miss," he said at last. He spoke so softly she had to lean forward to hear him. "She's been fed up and I'm worried about her and I don't know what to do ..."

He talked, and sometimes Miss Wilson asked a question, but mostly she just listened. After a while she got up and went to sit next to him.

"Never mind, Jayden," she said. "It sounds as if your mum has been having a rough time

and maybe needs some help. Would you like
me to see what I can do?"

Jayden looked up and nodded. Then he
smiled for the first time that day.

After a while Miss Wilson sent him out
to play. She sat at her desk for a moment,
working out a plan. Get Jayden's mum in for a
chat, maybe see if there was anyone who could

help her ... Miss Wilson knew she would also have to make sure Jayden and his sister got some help as well.

Now Miss Wilson smiled too. She had made up her mind. She wouldn't be able to do all those things if she wasn't a teacher any more, would she? She would have to stick with it for the time being, if she wanted to help Jayden. She couldn't do magic, but if she was Jayden's teacher she could help him at school and tell Mrs Green that his mum needed some support. That might change things.

She headed for the staff room to tell Mrs Green she wanted to stay after all.

*

That afternoon passed quickly for Jayden. There was some whispering about what had happened at lunch-time, but Miss Wilson soon put a stop to it. She got them to do some more work on their Vikings topic but then said they could read quietly.

Jayden had been stuck on the same book for a long time, and he didn't get much further with it now. He was too busy going over in his mind what had happened, the third surprise of his day – Miss Wilson offering to help him with his mum. Of course he'd said yes. He wasn't stupid, and he knew he needed some grown-up help. He wasn't sure what Miss Wilson would be able to do, but he felt he could trust her.

But he was never going to trust Dylan again. Jayden knew Dylan felt bad because of what had happened at lunch-time – Dylan wasn't talking to Luca any more and he kept looking over at Jayden instead. Luca didn't care – there was always someone he could get to be his friend because of all the cool stuff he had. But Jayden didn't much care either. He was sure he would soon have a much better friend than Dylan.

"Would you like to swap books with me?" whispered the boy sitting next to him. It was Olufemi, of course. "I've just finished mine, and I think you might like it."

"OK, thanks," said Jayden, and handed his book over. The one Olufemi swapped with him had a really good cover – an exciting picture of a young Viking.

"Er ... would you like to come to my house after school?" said Olufemi.

"Sorry, I don't think I can today," said Jayden. "But I could tomorrow."

"Ssshh!" Kasia hissed. "This is supposed to be a quiet time for reading!"

"That's fine," said Olufemi, and they turned to their books.

Jayden would have loved to go to Olufemi's house after school today, but he knew he had to take Madison home and make sure Mum was all right. When he thought about his mum, he started to feel sick with worry again.

*

Home time came at last. Madison waited for Jayden with Miss Patel in her classroom and Jayden went to collect her. She was OK. She'd got over what had happened at lunch, but she held tight to Jayden's hand as they set off for home.

Twenty minutes later they were standing in front of their door. Jayden opened it with his key and they went inside. There was a strange smell in the flat. Jayden couldn't work out what it was at first, then he clicked – Mum had done the washing.

"Hello, you two," Mum said, stepping out of the kitchen. "Have you had a good day? I'm really sorry about this morning, I just haven't been myself these last few weeks ..."

Jayden and Madison looked at each other, and then they both hugged her.

"That's OK, Mum," Jayden said. "I'm sure everything is going to be fine."

Maybe it hadn't been such a bad day after all.

Our books are tested
for children and young people by
children and young people.

Thanks to everyone who consulted on
a manuscript for their time and effort in
helping us to make our books better
for our readers.